Copyright © 2000 by NordSüd Verlag AG, Gossau Zürich, Switzerland
First published in Switzerland under the title *Wer fährt mit ans Meer?*
English translation copyright © 2000 by North-South Books Inc.

First published in the United States, Great Britain, Canada, Australia,
and New Zealand in 2000 by North-South Books,
an imprint of NordSüd Verlag AG, Gossau Zürich, Switzerland.
First paperback edition published in 2003 by North-South Books.
Distributed in the United States by North-South Books Inc., New York.

A CIP catalogue record for this book is available from The British Library.

Library of Congress Cataloging-in-Publication Data
Luciani, Brigitte.
[*Wer fährt mit ans Meer? English*]
How will we get to the beach?/Brigitte Luciani; illustrated by Eve Tharlet.
p. cm.
"A Michael Neugebauer book."
Summary: The reader is asked to guess what Roxanne must leave behind
(ball, umbrella, book, turtle, or baby) as she tries various means of
transportation to get to the beach.
[1. Beaches—Fiction. 2. Transportation—Fiction.] I. Tharlet, Eve, ill. II. Title.
PZ7.L9713 Ho 2000   [E]—dc21   99-057086

ISBN-13: 978-0-7358-1268-0 / ISBN-10: 0-7358-1268-3 (trade edition) 10 9 8 7 6 5 4 3
ISBN-13: 978-0-7358-1783-8 / ISBN-10: 0-7358-1783-9 (paperback edition) 10 9 8 7 6 5 4 3 2

Printed in Germany

A MICHAEL NEUGEBAUER BOOK
NORTH-SOUTH BOOKS / NEW YORK / LONDON

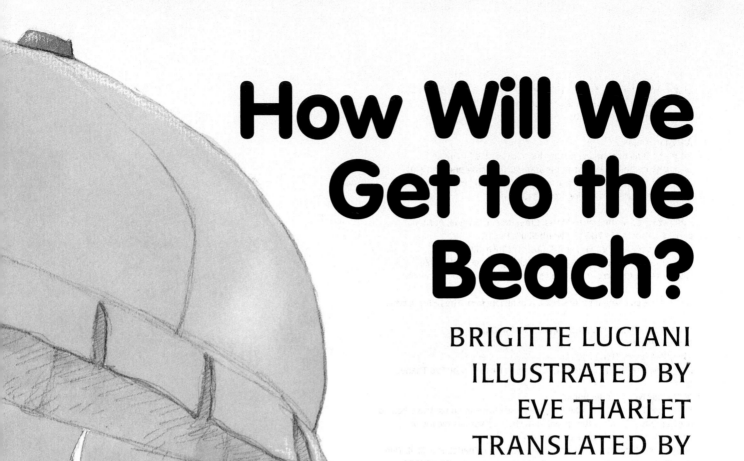

How Will We Get to the Beach?

BRIGITTE LUCIANI
ILLUSTRATED BY
EVE THARLET
TRANSLATED BY
ROSEMARY LANNING

One beautiful summer
day Roxanne decided to
go to the beach.
Everything she wanted to
take with her could be
counted on the fingers
of one hand:

the turtle,
the umbrella,
the thick book
of stories,
the ball, and,
of course, her baby.

But the car wouldn't start.

"Then we'll take the bus to the beach," said Roxanne.

But something couldn't go
with them. What was it?

The little green turtle!

Animals weren't allowed on the bus.
"We can't go to the beach without the turtle!"
cried Roxanne.

"Then we'll ride our bike to the beach," she said.

But something couldn't go with them. What was it?

The orange-spotted ball!

The ball wouldn't fit on the bicycle.
"We can't go to the beach without the ball!"
cried Roxanne.

"Then we'll ride our skateboard to the beach," she said.

But something couldn't go with them. What was it?

The big yellow umbrella.

Roxanne didn't have a free hand to hold it.
"We can't go to the beach without the umbrella!"
cried Roxanne.

"Then we'll ride our kayak to the beach," she said.

But something couldn't go with them. What was it?

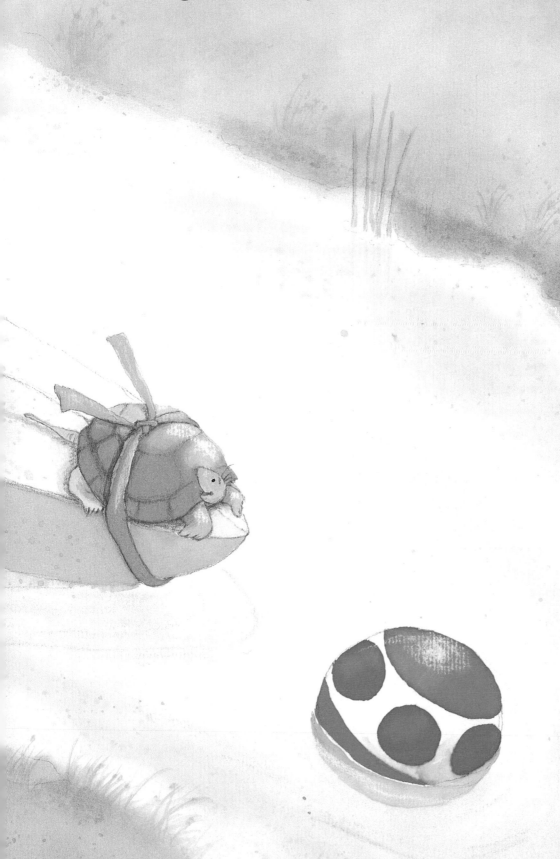

The thick blue book of stories.

The kayak was very wobbly, and the book might get wet.
"We can't go to the beach without the book!"
cried Roxanne.

"Then we'll fly in a balloon to the beach," she said.

But something couldn't go with them. What was it?

Roxanne's baby!

He wouldn't climb aboard because he was afraid of flying.
"We can't go to the beach without my baby!" cried Roxanne. "He is more important than all the other things. I wouldn't go anywhere without my baby!"

Roxanne sighed. "How will we *ever* get to the beach?"

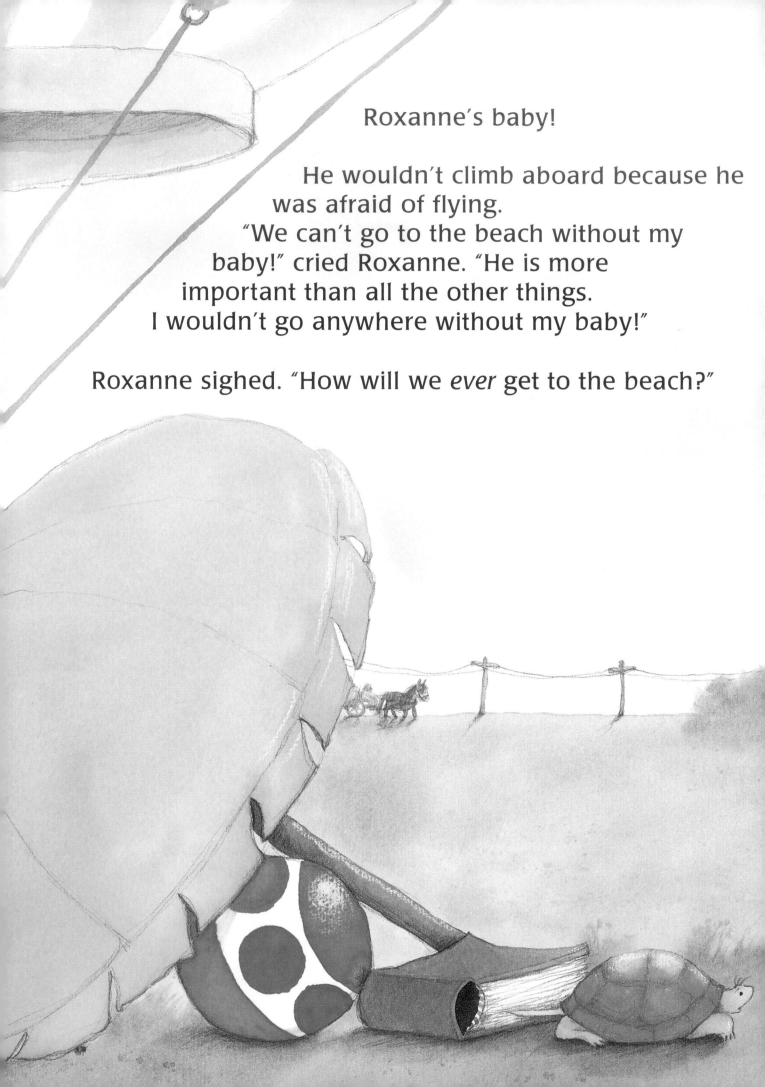

Just then a farmer passed by with his horse and cart.
He was on his way to the beach to sell cherries.

So they piled aboard:
Roxanne,
the green turtle,
the big yellow umbrella,
the thick blue book of stories,
the orange-spotted ball,
and, of course, her baby.

And they had a wonderful time!